THE LAST RAKOSH

F. PAUL WILSON

THE
LAST
RAKOSH

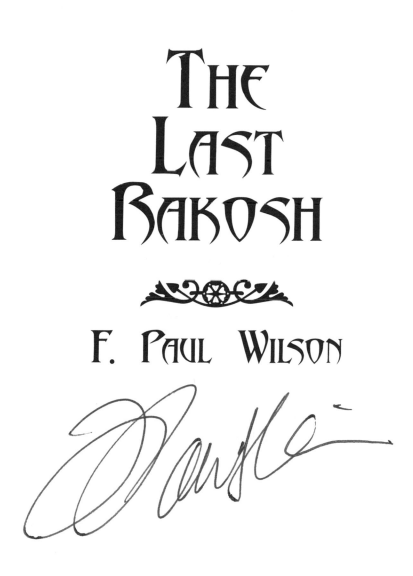

F. PAUL WILSON

OVERLOOK CONNECTION PRESS

2005

THE LAST RAKOSH
2005 © by F. Paul WIlson

Dust Jacket illustration © 2005 by Rick Sardinha

Published by
Overlook Connection Press
PO Box 1934, Hiram, Georgia 30141
www.overlookconnection.com
overlookcn@aol.com

Trade Hardcover ISBN: 1-892950-7-58

A signed limited hard cover of 500 copies
is available from OCP and Specialty Bookstores.
You can view complete details at:
www.overlookconnection.com/ocpmain.htm

First Edition

Book Design & Typesetting:
David G. Barnett/Fat Cat Design

THE
LAST
RAKOSH

I

"I don't know about this," Gia said as they stood outside the entrance to the main tent. A faded red-and-yellow banner flapped in the breeze.

THE OZYMANDIAS PRATHER
ODDITY EMPORIUM

Jack checked out the sparse queue passing through the entrance: A varied crew running the gamut from middle-class folk who looked like they'd just come from church to Goth types in full black regalia. But nobody looked threatening.

"What's wrong?"

"It looks like some sort of freak show." She

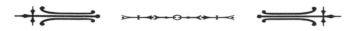

glanced quickly at Vicky, then at Jack. "I just don't know."

Her meaning was clear.

"Truth is, I'm having second thoughts myself."

"You?" Gia's faint, pale eyebrows lifted. "If the most politically incorrect man I know is hesitating, we'd better turn around and go home."

Jack had seen a flyer for the show and thought this might be a unique experience for Vicks, an exhibit of weird objects and odd people doing strange tricks—sort of like a bunch of Letterman's "Stupid People Tricks" under one roof. But he didn't want to take an eight-year-old girl to a freak show. The very idea of deformed people putting themselves on display repulsed him. It was demeaning, and people who paid to gawk seemed to come off as demeaned as the freaks on display. Maybe more so. He didn't want to be one of them.

"Go home?" Vicky said. "I thought we came out to see the show."

"I know, Vicky," Gia began, "but it's just that—"

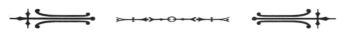

"You said we were going!" Her voice started pitching toward a whine. She turned to Jack with a hurt look. "Jack, you said! You said we were gonna see neat stuff!"

Vicky was very good with that look. She knew it wielded almost limitless power over Jack.

"You might be scared by some of the things in there," he told her.

"You promised, Jack!"

He hadn't actually promised, not in so many words, but the implication had been there. He looked to Gia for help, but she seemed to be waiting for him to make a decision.

"Well," he said to Gia, "I think she'll be all right." When Gia's eyebrows lifted again, he added, "Hey, I figure after what she went through last summer, nothing in there's going to scare her."

Gia sighed. "Good point."

Jack led them to the ticket booth where he forked over a twenty.

"One adult, two children, please."

The guy in the booth, a beefy type sporting a straw boater, looked around.

"I see two adults and one kid."

"Yeah, but I'm a kid at heart."

"Funny."

With no hint of a smile, Mr. Ticket slid two adults and one child plus change across the tray.

Inside, the show seemed pretty shabby and Jack wondered if they'd been had. Everything looked so worn, from the signs above the booths to the poles supporting the canvas. Glance up and it was immediately apparent from the sunlight leaking through the canvas that the Oddity Emporium was in dire need of new tents. He wondered what they did when it rained. Thunderstorms were predicted for later. Jack was glad they'd be out of here and on their way back home long before.

As they strolled along, Jack tried to classify the Ozymandias Prather Oddity Emporium. Yeah, a freak show in some ways, but in many ways not.

First off, Jack had never seen freaks like some of these. Sure, they had the World's Fattest Man, a giant billed as the World's Tallest Man, two sisters with

undersized heads who sang in piercing falsetto harmony—nothing so special about them.

Then they came to the others.

By definition freaks were supposed to be strange, but these folk went beyond strange into the positively alien. The Alligator Boy, the Bird Man with flapping feathered wings…

"Did you see the Snake Man back there?" Gia whispered as they trailed behind the utterly enthralled Vicky.

Jack nodded. These "freaks" were so alien they couldn't be real human beings.

"Got to be a fake," he said. "Make up and prosthetics."

"That's what I thought, but I couldn't see where the real him ended and the fake began. And did you see the way he used his tail to wrap around that stuffed rabbit and squeeze it? Almost like a boa constrictor."

"A good fake, but still a fake." Had to be.

One aspect of the show that reinforced his sense of fakery was that there was nothing the least bit sad or pathetic about these "freaks." No matter how bizarre their bodies, they seemed proud of their deformities—almost belligerently so. As if the people strolling the midway were the freaks.

Jack and Gia caught up to Vicky where she'd stopped before a midget standing on a miniature throne. He had a tiny handlebar mustache and slicked-down black hair parted in the middle. A gold-lettered sign hung above him: *Little Sir Echo*.

"Hi!" Vicky said.

"Hi, yourself," the little man replied in a note-perfect imitation of Vicky's voice.

"Hey, Mom!" Vicky cried. "He sounds just like me!"

"Hey, Mom!" Little Sir Echo said. "Come on over and listen to this guy!"

Jack noticed a tension in Gia's smile and thought he knew why. The mimicked voice was too much like Vicky's—pitch and timbre, all perfect down to the subtlest nuance. If Jack had been facing away, he wouldn't have had the slightest doubt that Vicky had spoken.

Amazing, but creepy too.

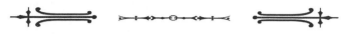

"You're very good," Gia said.

"I'm not very good," he replied in a perfect imitation of Gia's voice. "I'm the best. And your voice is as beautiful as you are."

Gia flushed. "Why, thank you."

The midget turned to Jack, still speaking in Gia's voice: "And you, sir— Mr. Strong Silent Type. Care to say anything?"

"Yoo doorty rat!" Jack said in his best imitation of a bad comic imitating James Cagney. "Yoo killed my brutha!"

Gia burst out laughing. "God, Jack, that's awful!"

"A W. C. Fields fan!" the little man cried with a mischievous wink. "I have an old recording of one of his stage acts! Want to hear?"

Without waiting for a reply, Sir Echo began to mimic the record, and a chill ran through Jack as he realized that the little man was faithfully reproducing not only the voice, but the pops and cracks of the scratched vinyl as well.

"Marvelous, my good man!" Jack said

in a W.C. Fields imitation as bad as his Cagney. "But now we must take our leave. We're off to Philadelphia, you know."

"You should stick to your own voice," Gia said as Jack guided her away from the booth.

Jack didn't tell her that something in a pre-rational corner of his brain had been afraid to let the midget hear his natural voice. Probably the same something that made jungle tribal folk shun a camera for fear it would steal their souls.

"Look!" Vicky said, pointing to the far end of the midway. "Cotton candy! Can I have some?"

"Sure," Gia said. "You go ahead and pick the color and we'll be right there."

Jack smiled as he watched her go. Always good to give Vicky a head start if decisions such as shape and color were involved. She agonized over those sorts of minutiae.

As they passed a booth with a green-skinned fellow billed as "The Man from Mars," Gia took Jack's hand.

"Vicky seems to be having a great

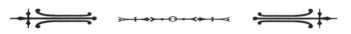

time." She leaned against him. "And to tell the truth, I'm kind of enjoying this myself."

Jack was about to reply when a child's scream pierced them, froze them.

Jack looked at Gia and saw the panic in her eyes. It came again, unquestionably Vicky's voice, high-pitched, quavering with terror.

Jack was already moving toward the sound, traveling as fast as the crowd would permit, bumping and pushing those he couldn't slide past. But where was she? She'd been moving ahead of them down the midway only a moment ago. How far could she have gone in less than a minute?

Then he spotted her skinny eight-year-old form darting toward him, her face a strained mask of white, her blue eyes wide with fear. When she saw him she burst into tears and held out her arms as she stumbled toward him. Her voice was a shriek.

"Jack! Jack! It's back! It's gonna get me again!"

She leaped and he caught her, holding her tight as she quaked with fear.

"What is it, Vicks? What's the matter?"

"The monster! The monster that took me to the boat! It's here! Don't let it get me!"

"It's okay, it's okay," he said soothingly in her ear. "No one can hurt you when I'm around."

Out of the corner of his eye he saw Gia hurrying toward them. He gently peeled Vicky off and transferred her to her mother. Vicky immediately wrapped her arms and legs around Gia.

Gia's expression fluctuated between fear and anger. "My God, what happened?"

"I think she believes she saw a rakosh."

Gia's eyes widened. "But that's—"

"Impossible. Right. But maybe she saw something that looks like one."

"No!" Vicky cried from where her face was buried against her mother's neck. "It's the one that took me! I *know* it is!"

"Okay, Vicks." Jack gave her trembling back a gentle rub. "I'll check it out." He

nodded to Gia. "Why don't you take her outside."

"We're on our way. After what I've seen here, I wouldn't be half surprised if she was right."

Jack watched Gia slip through the crowd, holding her daughter tight against her. When they were out of sight he turned and headed in the direction Vicky had come.

Wouldn't be half surprised myself, he thought.

Not that there was a single chance in hell of one of Kusum's rakoshi being alive. They'd all died last summer in the water between Governor's Island and the Battery. He'd seen to that. His incendiary bombs had crisped them in the hold of the ship that housed them. One of them did make it to shore, the one he'd dubbed Scar-lip, but it had swum back out into the burning water and never returned.

The rakoshi were dead. All of them. The species was extinct.

Next to a stall containing a woman with a third eye in the center of her forehead that supposedly "Sees ALL!" sat an old circus cart with iron bars on its open side, one of the old cages-on-wheels once used to transport and display lions and tigers and such. The sign above it said "The Amazing Sharkman!" Jack noticed people leaning across the rope border; they'd peer into the cage, then back off with uneasy shrugs.

This deserved a look.

Jack pushed to the front and squinted into the dimly lit cage. Something slumped in the left rear corner, head down, chin on chest, immobile. Something huge, a seven-footer at least. Dark-skinned, man-like and yet... undeniably alien.

Jack felt the skin along the back of his neck tighten as ripples of warning shot down his spine. He knew that shape. But that was all it was. A shape. So immobile. It had to be a dummy of some sort, or a guy in a costume. A damn good costume. No wonder Vicky had been terrified.

But it couldn't be the real thing. Couldn't be...

Jack ducked under the rope and took a

few tentative steps closer to the cage, sniffing the air. One of the things he remembered about the rakoshi was their reek, like rotting meat. He caught a trace of it here, but that could have been from spilled garbage. Nothing like the breath-clogging stench he remembered.

He moved close enough to touch the bars but didn't. The thing was a damn good dummy. He could almost swear it was breathing.

Jack whistled and said, "Hey you in there!"

The thing didn't budge, so he rapped on one of the iron bars.

"Hey—!"

Suddenly it moved, the eyes snapping open as the head came up, deep yellow eyes that almost seemed to glow in the shadows.

Imagine the offspring of a tryst between a giant hairless gorilla and a mako shark: cobalt skin, hugely muscled, no neck worth mentioning, no external ears, narrow slits for a nose.

Spike-like talons, curved for tearing,

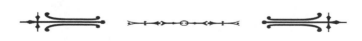

emerged from the tips of the three thick fingers on each hand as the yellow eyes fixed on Jack. The lower half of its huge shark-like head seemed to split as the jaw opened to reveal rows of razor-sharp teeth. It uncoiled its legs and slithered across the metal flooring toward the front of the cage.

Along with the instinctive revulsion, memories surged back: the cargo hold full of their dark shapes and glowing eyes, the unearthly chant, the disappearances, the deaths…

Jack backed up a step. Two. Behind him he heard the crowd "Oooh!" and "Aaah!" as it pressed forward for a better look. He took still another step back until he could feel their excited breaths on his neck. These people didn't know what one of these things could do, didn't know their power, their near indestructibility. Otherwise they'd be running the other way.

Jack felt his heart kick up its already rising tempo when he noticed the wide scar distorting the creature's lower lip. He knew this particular rakosh. Scar-lip. The one that had kidnapped Vicky, the one that had

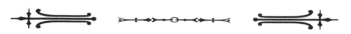

escaped the ship and almost got to Vicky on the shore. The one that had almost killed Jack.

He ran a hand across his chest. Even through the fabric of his shirt he could feel the three long ridges that ran across his chest, souvenir scars from this thing's talons.

His mouth felt like straw. Scar-lip… alive.

But *how*? How had it survived the blaze on the water? How had it wound up on Long Island in a traveling freak show?

"Ooh, look at it, Fred!" said a woman behind Jack.

"Just a guy in a rubber suit," said a supremely confident male voice.

"But those claws—did you see the way they came out?"

"Simple hydraulics. Nothing to it."

You go on believing that, Fred, Jack thought as he watched the creature where it crouched on its knees, its talons encircling the iron bars, its yellow eyes burning into him.

You know me too, don't you.

It appeared to be trying to stand but its legs wouldn't support it. Was it chained, or possibly maimed?

The ticket seller came by then, sans boater, revealing a shaven head. His cold dark eyes gleamed with a strange glee. He carried a blunt elephant gaff that he rapped against the bars.

"So you're up, ay?" he said to the rakosh in a harsh voice. "Maybe you've finally learned your lesson."

Jack noticed that for the first time since it had opened its eyes the rakosh turned its glare from him; it refocused on the new-comer.

"Here he is ladies and gentleman," the ticket man cried, turning to the crowd. "Yessir, the one and only Sharkman! The only one of his kind! He's exclusively on display here at Ozymandias Oddities. Tell your friends, tell your enemies. Yessir, you've never seen anything like him and never will anywhere else. Guaranteed."

You've got that right, Jack thought.

The ticket man spotted Jack standing on the wrong side of the rope. "Here, you.

Get back there. This thing's dangerous! See those claws? One swipe and you'd be sliced up like a tomato by a Ginsu knife! We don't want to see our customers get sliced up." His eyes said otherwise as he none too gently prodded Jack with the pole. "Back now."

Jack slipped under the rope, never taking his eyes off Scar-lip. The rakosh didn't look well. Its skin was dull, and relatively pale, nothing like the shiny deep cobalt he remembered from their last meeting. It looked thin, almost wasted.

Scar-lip turned its attention from the ticket man and stared at Jack a moment longer, then dropped its gaze. Its talons retracted, slipping back inside the fingertips, the arms dropped to its sides, the shoulders drooped, then it turned and crawled back to the rear of the cage where it slumped again in the corner and hung its head.

Drugged. That had to be the answer. They had to tranquilize the rakosh to keep it manageable. Even so, it didn't look too healthy. Maybe the iron bars were doing

it—fire and iron, the only things that could hurt a rakosh.

But drugged or not, healthy or not, Scar-lip had recognized Jack, remembered him. Which meant it could remember Vicky. And if it ever got free, it might come after Vicky again, to complete the task its dead master had set for it.

The ticket man began banging on the rakosh's cage in a fury, screaming at it to get up and face the crowd. But the creature ignored him, and the crowd began to wander off in search of more active attractions.

Jack turned and headed for the exit. A cold resolve had overtaken his initial shock. He knew what had to be done.

2

It was late when Jack parked at the edge of the marsh on a rutted road. It ended a few hundred yards farther out at a tiny shack sitting alone near the Long Island Sound. He wondered who lived there.

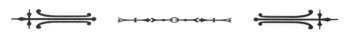

A mist had formed, hugging the ground. The shack looked ominous and lonely floating in the fog out there with its single lighted window. Reminded Jack of an old gothic paperback cover.

He stuck his head out the window. Only a sliver of moon above, but plenty of stars. Enough light to get him where he wanted to go without a flashlight. He could make out the grassy area the Oddity Emporium used for parking. Only one or two cars there. As he watched, their headlights came alive and moved off in the direction of town.

Business was slow, it seemed. Good. The show would be bedding down early.

After the lights went out and things had been quiet for a while, Jack slipped out of the car and took a two-gallon can from the trunk. Gasoline sloshed within as he strode across the uneven ground toward the hulking silhouette of the main show tent. The performers' and hands' trailers stood off to the north side by a big eighteen-wheel truck.

No security in sight. Jack slipped under

the canvas sidewall and listened. Quiet. A couple of incandescent bulbs had been left on, one hanging from the ceiling every thirty feet or so. Keeping to the shadows along the side, Jack made his way behind the booths toward Scar-lip's cage.

His plan was simple: Flood the floor of the rakosh's cage and douse the thing itself with the gas, then strike a match. Normally the idea of immolating a living creature would sicken him, but this was a rakosh. If a bullet in the brain would have done the trick, he'd have come fully loaded. But the only sure way to off a rakosh was fire…the cleansing flame.

Jack knew from experience that once a rakosh started to burn, it was quickly consumed. As soon as he was sure the flames were doing their thing, he'd run for the trailers shouting "Fire!" at the top of his lungs, then dash for his car.

He just hoped the performers and roustabouts would arrive with their extinguishers in time to keep the whole tent from going up.

He didn't like this, didn't like endan-

gering the tent or anybody nearby, but it was the only scheme he could come up with on such short notice. He would protect Vicky at any cost, and this was the only sure way he knew.

He approached the "Sharkman" area warily from the blind end, then made a wide circle around to the front. Scar-lip was stretched out on the floor of the cage, sleeping, its right arm dangling through the bars. It opened its eyes as he neared. Their yellow was even duller than this afternoon. Its talons extended only part way as it made a half-hearted, almost perfunctory swipe in Jack's direction. Then it closed its eyes and let the arm dangle again. It didn't seem to have strength or the heart for anything more.

Jack stopped and stared at the creature. And he knew.

It's dying.

He stood there a long time and watched Scar-lip doze in its cage. Was it sick or was something else ailing it? Some animals couldn't live outside a pack. Jack had destroyed this thing's nest and all its

brothers and sisters along with it. Was this last rakosh dying of loneliness, or had it simply reached the end of its days? What was the life-span of a rakosh, anyway?

Jack shifted the gas can in his hands and wondered if he was needed here. He'd torch a vital, aggressive, healthy rakosh without a qualm, because he knew if positions were reversed it would tear off his head without a second thought. But it seemed a pretty sure bet that Scar-lip would be history before long. So why endanger the carny folk with a fire?

On the other hand…what if Scar-lip recovered and got free? It was a possibility. And he'd never forgive himself if it came after Vicky again. Jack had damn near died saving Vicky the last time—and he'd been lucky at that. Could he count on that kind of luck again?

Uh-uh. Never count on luck.

He began unscrewing the cap of the gasoline can but stopped when he heard voices…coming this way down the midway. He ducked for the shadows.

"I tell you, Hank," said a voice that

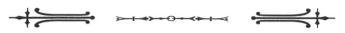

sounded familiar, "you should've seen the big wimp this afternoon. Something got it riled. It had the crowd six deep around its cage while it was up."

Jack recognized the bald-headed ticket seller who'd prodded him back behind the rope this afternoon. The other man with him was taller, younger, but just as beefy, with a full head of sandy hair. He carried a bottle of what looked like cheap wine while the bald one carried a six-foot iron bar, sharpened at one end. Neither of them was walking too steadily.

"Maybe we taught it a good lesson last night, huh, Bondy?" said the one called Hank.

"Just lesson number one," Bondy said. "The first of many. Yessir, the first of many."

They stopped before the cage. Bondy took a swig from the bottle and handed it back to Hank.

"Look at it," Bondy said. "The big blue wimp. Thinks it can just sit around all day and sleep all night. No way, babe! Y'gotta earn your keep, wimp!" He took the sharp

end of the iron bar and jabbed it at the rakosh. "*Earn* it!"

The point pierced Scar-lip's shoulder. The creature moaned like a cow with laryngitis and rolled away. The bald guy kept jabbing at it, stabbing its back again and again, making it moan while Hank stood by, grinning.

Jack turned and crept off through the shadows. The two carnies had found the only other thing that could harm a rakosh—iron. Fire and iron—they were impervious to everything else. Maybe that was another explanation for Scar-lip's poor health—caged with iron bars.

As Jack moved away, he heard Hank's voice rise over the tortured cries of the dying rakosh.

"When's it gonna be my turn, Bondy? Huh? When's my turn?"

The hoarse moans followed Jack out into the night. He stowed the can back in the trunk, and got as far as opening the car door. Then he stopped.

"Shit!" he said and pounded the roof of the car. "Shit! Shit! *Shit!*"

He slammed the door closed and trotted back to the freak show tent, repeating the word all the way.

No stealth this time. He strode directly to the section he'd just left, pulled up the sidewall, and charged inside. Bondy still had the iron pike—or maybe he had it back again. Jack stepped up beside him just as he was preparing for another jab at the trapped, huddled creature. He snatched the pike from his grasp.

"That's enough, asshole."

Bondy looked at him wide-eyed, his forehead wrinkling up to where his hairline should have been. Probably no one had talked to him that way in a long, long time.

"Who the fuck are you?"

"Nobody you want to know right now. Maybe you should call it a night."

Bondy took a swing at Jack's face. He telegraphed it by baring his teeth. Jack raised the rod between his face and the fist. Bondy screamed as his knuckles smashed against the iron, then did a knock-kneed walk in a circle with the hand jammed between his thighs, groaning in pain.

Suddenly a pair of arms wrapped around Jack's torso, trapping him in a fleshy vise.

"I got him, Bondy!" Hank's voice shouted from behind Jack's left ear. "I got him!"

Twenty feet away, Bondy stopped his dance, looked up, and grinned. As he charged, Jack rammed his head backward, smashing the back of his skull into Hank's nose. Abruptly he was free. He still held the iron bar, so he angled the blunt end toward the charging Bondy and drove it hard into his solar plexus. The air *whooshed* out of him and he dropped to his knees with a groan, his face gray-green. Even his scalp looked sick.

Jack glanced up and saw Scar-lip crouched at the front of the cage, gripping the bars, its yellow gaze flicking between him and the groaning Bondy, but lingering on Jack, as if trying to comprehend what he was doing, and why. Tiny rivulets of dark blood trailed down its skin.

Jack whirled the pike 180 degrees and pressed the point against Bondy's chest.

"What kind of noise am I going to hear when I poke you with *this* end?"

Behind him Hank's voice, very nasal now, started shouting.

"Hey, Rube! Hey, Rube!"

As Jack was trying to figure out just what that meant, he gave the kneeling Bondy a poke with the pointed end—not enough to break the skin, but enough to scare him. He howled and fell back on the sawdust, screaming.

"Don't! Don't!"

Meanwhile, Hank had kept up his "Hey, Rube!" shouts. As Jack turned to shut him up, he found out what it meant.

The tent was filling with carny folk. Lots of them, all running his way. In seconds he was surrounded. The workers he could handle, but the others, the performers, gathered in a crowd like this in the murky light, in various states of dress, were unsettling. The Snake Man, the Alligator Boy, the Bird Man, the green man from Mars, and others were all still in costume— at least Jack hoped they were costumes— and none of them looked too friendly.

Hank was holding his bloody nose, wagging his finger at Jack. "Now you're gonna get it! *Now* you're gonna get it!"

Bondy seemed to have a sudden infusion of courage. He hauled himself to his feet and started toward Jack with a raised fist.

"You goddamn son of a—"

Jack rapped the iron bar across the side of his bald head, staggering him. With an angry murmur, the circle of carny folk abruptly tightened.

Jack whirled, spinning the pike around him. "Right," he said. "Who's next?"

He hoped it was a convincing show. He didn't know what else to do. He'd taken some training in the martial use of the bamboo pole and nunchuks and the like; he wasn't Bruce Lee with them, but he could do some damage with this pike. Trouble was, he had little room to maneuver, and less every second: the circle was tightening, slowly closing in on him like a noose.

Jack searched for a weak spot, a point to break through and make a run for it. As a last resort, he always had the .45 caliber Semmerling strapped to his ankle.

Then a deep voice rose above the angry noise of the crowd.

"Here, here! What's this? What's going on?"

The carny folk quieted, but not before Jack heard a few voices whisper "the boss" and "Oz." They parted to make way for a tall man, six-three at least, lank dark hair, sallow complexioned, his pear-shaped body swathed in a huge silk robe embroidered with Oriental designs. Although he looked doughy about the middle, the large hands that protruded from his sleeves were thin and bony at the wrist.

The boss—Jack assumed he was the Ozymandias Prather who ran the show—stopped at the inner edge of the circle and took in the scene. His expression was oddly slack but his eyes were bright, dark, cold, more alive than the rest of him. Those eyes finally settled on Jack.

"Who are you and what are you doing here?"

"Protecting your property," Jack said, gambling.

"Oh, really?" The smile was sour.

"How magnanimous of you." Abruptly his expression darkened. "Answer the question! I can call the police or we can deal with this in our own way."

"Fine," Jack said. He upped his ante by throwing the pike at the boss's feet. "Maybe I had it wrong. Maybe you *pay* baldy here to poke holes in your attractions."

The big man froze for an instant, then slowly wheeled toward the ticket seller who was rubbing the welt on the side of his head.

"Hey, boss—" Bondy began, but the tall man silenced him with a flick of his hand.

The boss looked down at the pike where sawdust clung to the dark fluid coating its point, then up at the crouching rakosh with its dozens of oozing wounds. Color darkened his cheeks as his head rotated back toward Bondy.

"You harmed this creature, Mr. Bond?"

The boss's eyes and tone were so full of menace that Jack couldn't blame the bald man for quailing.

"We was only trying to get it to put on more of a show for the customers."

Jack glanced around and noticed that Hank had faded away. He saw the performers inching toward the rakosh cage, making sympathetic sounds as they took in its condition. When they turned back, their cold stares were focused on Bondy instead of Jack.

"You hurt him," said the green man.

"He is our brother," the snake man said in a soft sibilant voice, "and you hurt him many times."

Brother? Jack wondered. What are they talking about? What's going on here?

The boss continued to pin Bondy with his glare. "And you feel you can get more out of the creature by mistreating it?"

"We thought—"

"I know what you thought, Mr. Bond. And many of us know too well how the Sharkman felt. We've all known mistreatment during the course of our lives, and we don't look kindly upon it. You will retire to your quarters immediately and wait for me there."

"Fuck that!" Bondy said. "And fuck you, Oz! I'm blowin' the show! Ain't goin' nowhere but outta here!"

The boss gestured to the alligator boy and the bird man. "Escort Mr. Bond to my trailer. See that he waits outside until I get there."

Bondy tried to duck through the crowd but the green man blocked his way until the other two grabbed his arms. He struggled but was no match for them.

"You can't do this, Oz!" he shouted, fear wild in his eyes as he was none too gently dragged away. "You can't keep me here if I wanna go!"

Oz ignored him and turned his attention to Jack. "And that leaves us with you, Mr...?"

"Jack."

"Jack what?"

"Just Jack."

"Very well, Mr. Jack. What is your interest in this matter?"

"I don't like bullies."

It wasn't an answer, but it would have to do. Wasn't about to tell the boss he'd come to French fry his Sharkman.

"Does anyone? But why should you be interested in this particular creature? Why should you be here at all?"

"Not too often you get to see a real live rakosh."

When he saw the boss blink and snap his head toward the cage, Jack had a sudden uneasy feeling that he'd made a mistake. How big a mistake, he wasn't quite sure.

"What did you say?" The glittering eyes fixed on him again. "What did you call it?"

"Nothing," Jack said.

"No, I heard you. You called it a rakosh." Oz stepped over to the cage and stared into Scar-lip's yellow eyes. "Is that what you are, my friend...a rakosh? How fascinating!" He turned to the rest of his employees. "It's all right. You can all go back to bed. Everything is under control. I wish to speak to this gentleman in private before he goes."

"You didn't know what it was?" Jack said as the crowd dispersed.

Oz continued to stare at the rakosh. "Not until this moment. I thought they were a myth."

"How did you find it?" Jack said. The

answer was important—until this afternoon he'd been sure he'd killed Scar-lip.

"The result of a telephone call.
Someone phoned me last summer—woke
me in the middle of the night—and told me
that if I searched the waters off Governors
Island I might find 'a fascinating new
attraction.'"

Last summer…the last time he'd seen
Scar-lip and the rest of his species. "Who
called you? Was it a woman?"

"No. Why do you ask?"

"Just wondering."

Besides Gia, Vicky, Abe, and himself,
the only other living person who knew
about the rakoshi had been Kolabati.

"Something in the caller's voice, his
utter conviction, compelled me to do as he
said. Came the dawn I was on the water
with some of my people. We found our-
selves vying with groups of
souvenir-hunters looking for wreckage
from a ship that had exploded and burned
the night before. We discovered our friend
here floating in a clump of debris. I
assumed the creature was dead, but when I

found it was alive, I had it brought ashore. It looked rather vicious so I put it into an old tiger cage."

"Lucky for you."

The boss smiled, showing yellow teeth. "I should say so. It almost tore the cage apart. But since then its health has followed a steady downhill course. We've offered it fish, fowl, beef, horse meat, even vegetables—although one look at those teeth and there's no question that it's a carnivore—but no matter what we've tried, its health continues to fail."

Jack now had an idea why Scar-lip was dying. Rakoshi required a very specific species of flesh to thrive. And this one wasn't getting it.

"I brought in a veterinary expert," Oz went on, "one I have learned to rely on for his discretion, but he could not alter the creature's downhill course."

"Well..." Jack said, trying to sound tentative. "I saw a picture of one in a book once. I...I *think* it looked like this. But I'm not sure. I could be wrong."

"But you're *not* wrong," the boss said,

turning and staring into his eyes. He lowered his gaze to Jack's chest, fixing on the area where the rakosh had scarred him. "And I believe you have far more intimate knowledge of this creature than you are willing to admit."

Jack shrugged, uncomfortable with the scrutiny, especially since it wasn't the first time someone had stared at his chest this way.

"But it doesn't matter!" Oz laughed and spread his arms. "A rakosh! How wonderful! And it's all mine!"

Jack glanced at Scar-lip's slouched, wasted form. Yeah, but not for long.

He heard a noise like a growl and turned. The sight of one of the burly roustabouts standing in the exit flap startled him. He looked like he was waving good bye to his boss.

"Excuse me," Oz said and hurried toward the exit, his silk robe fluttering around him.

Jack turned to find Scar-lip staring at him with its cold yellow eyes. Still want to finish me off, don't you. It's mutual, pal.

But it looks like I'm going to outlast you by a few years. A few *decades*.

The longer he remained with the wasted creature, the more convinced he was that Scar-lip was on its last legs. He didn't have to light him up. The creature was a goner.

Jack kept tabs on Oz out of the corner of his eye. After half a minute of hushed, one-sided conversation—all the employee did was nod every so often—the boss man returned.

"Sorry. I had to revise instructions on an important errand. But I do want to thank you. You have provided a bright moment in a very disappointing stop." His gaze drifted. "Usually we do extremely well in Monroe, but this trip…it seems a house disappeared last month—vanished, foundation and all, amid strange flashing lights one night. The locals are still spooked."

"How about that," Jack said, turning away. "I think I'll be going."

"But you must allow me to reward you for succoring the poor creature, and for identifying it. Free passes, perhaps."

"Not necessary," Jack said and headed for the exit.

"By the way," Oz said. "How can I get in touch with you if I wish?"

Jack called back over his shoulder. "You can't."

A final glance at Scar-lip showed the rakosh still staring at him, then he parted the canvas flaps and emerged into the fresh air again.

A strange mix of emotions swirled around him as he returned to the car. Glad to know Scar-lip would be taking a dirt nap soon, but the very fact that it still lived, even if it was too weak to be a threat to Vicky, bothered him. He'd prefer it dead. He'd keep a close watch on this show, check back every night or two until he knew without a doubt that Scar-lip had breathed its last.

Something else bothered him. Couldn't put his finger on it, but he had this vaguely uncomfortable feeling that he never should have come back here.

3

The following night Jack drove out to Monroe for another look at Scar-lip.

The rain started as soon as he stepped out of the car. It came in tropical style. One minute simply threatening, the next Jack was treading through a waterfall. He arrived at the gate soaked and mud splattered and in a foul mood. At least the main tent was still up, although the front flap was down and no one was selling tickets. Place looked pretty much deserted.

Jack slipped through the flap. The stale air trapped under the leaking canvas was redolent of wet hay and strange sweat. His feet squished within his wet deck shoes as he made his way toward Scar-lip's cage, but stopped short, stopped stone cold dead when he saw what was behind the bars.

Scar-lip, all right, but the creature he'd seen last night had been only the palest reflection of this monster. The rakosh rearing up in the cage and rattling the bars now was full of vitality and ferocity, had unmarred, glistening blue-black skin, and bright yellow eyes that glowed with a fierce inner light.

Jack stood mute and numb on the fringe, thinking, This is a nightmare, one that keeps repeating itself.

The once moribund rakosh was now fiercely alive, and it wanted *out*.

Suddenly it froze and Jack saw that it was looking his way. Its cold yellow basilisk glare fixed on him. He felt like a deer in the headlights of an eighteen wheeler.

He turned and hurried from the tent. Outside in the rain he looked around and saw a trailer with an OFFICE sign on the door. Its canvas awning was bellied with rain. Jack knocked.

He stepped back as the door swung out. Prather stood staring down at Jack.

"Who are you?"

"And hello to you too. I was here the other night. I'm the 'Hey, Rube' guy."

"Ah, yes. The defender of rakoshi. Jack, isn't it?"

"I want to talk to you about that rakosh."

Oz backed away. "Come in, come in."

Jack stepped up and inside, just far enough to get out from under the dripping awning. The rain paradiddled on the metal roof, and Jack knew he had about five minutes before the sound made him crazy.

"Have you seen it?" Oz's voice seemed to come from everywhere in the room. "Isn't it magnificent?"

"What did you do to it?"

Oz stared at him, as if genuinely puzzled. "Why, my good man, now that I know what it is, I know how to treat it. I looked up the proper care and feeding of rakoshi in one of my books on Bengali mythology, and acted appropriately."

Jack felt a chill. And it was not from his soaked clothing.

"What...just *what* did you feed it?"

The boss's large brown eyes looked guileless, and utterly remorseless. "Oh, this and that. Whatever the text recommended. You don't really believe for an instant that I was going to allow that magnificent creature to languish and die of malnutrition, do you? I assume you're familiar with—"

"I *know* what a rakosh needs to live."

"Do you now? Do you know everything about rakoshi?"

"No, of course not, but—"

"Then let us assume that I know more than you. Perhaps there is more than one way to keep them healthy. I see no need to discuss this with you or anyone else. Let us just say that it got exactly what it needed." His smile was scary. "And that it enjoyed the meal immensely."

Jack knew a rakosh ate only one thing. The question was: Who? He knew Prather would never tell him so he didn't waste breath asking.

Instead he said, "Do you have any idea what you're playing with here? Do you know what's going to happen to your little troupe when that thing gets loose? I've seen this one in action, and trust me, pal, it will tear you all to pieces."

"I assume you know that iron weakens it. The bars of its cage are iron; the roof, floor, and sides are lined with steel. It will not escape."

"Famous last words. So I take it there's

no way I can convince you to douse it with kerosene and strike a match."

The boss's face darkened as he rose from his chair.

"I advise you to put that idea out of your head, or you may wind up sharing the cage with the creature." He stepped closer to Jack and edged him outside. "You have been warned. Good day, sir."

He reached a long arm past Jack and pulled the door closed.

Jack stood outside a moment, realizing that a worst-case scenario had come true. A healthy Scar-lip…he couldn't let that go on. He still had the can of gasoline in the trunk of his car.

He'd come back later. One last time.

As he turned, he found someone standing behind him. His nose was fat and discolored; dark crescents had formed under each eye. The rain, a drizzle now, had darkened his sandy hair, plastering it to his scalp. He stared at Jack, his face a mask of rage.

"You're that guy, the one who got Bondy and me in trouble!"

Now Jack recognized him: the

roustabout from Sunday night. Hank. His breath reeked of cheap wine. He clutched a bottle in a paper bag. Probably Mad Dog.

"It's all your fault!" Hank shouted.

"You're absolutely right."

Jack began walking toward his car. He had no time for this dolt.

"Bondy was my only friend! He got fired because of you."

A little bell went *ting-a-ling*. Jack stopped, turned.

"Yeah? When did you see him last?"

"The other night—when you got him in trouble."

The bell was ringing louder.

"And you never saw him once after that? Not even to say good-bye?"

Hank shook his head. "Uh-uh. Boss kicked him right out. By sun-up he'd blown the show with all his stuff."

Jack remembered the rage in Oz's eyes that night when he'd looked from the wounded rakosh to Bondy. Jack was pretty sure now that the ringing in his head was a dinner bell.

"He was the only one around here who

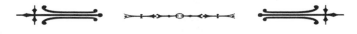

liked me," Hank said, his expression miserable. "Bondy talked to me. All the freaks and geeks keep to theirselves."

Jack sighed as he stared at Hank. Well, at least now he had an idea as to who had supplemented Scar-lip's diet.

No big loss to civilization.

"You don't need friends like that, kid," he said and turned away again.

"You'll pay for it!" Hank screamed into the rain. "Bondy'll be back and when he gets here we'll get even. I got my pay docked because of you and that damn Sharkman! You think you look bad now, you just wait till Bondy gets back!"

Pardon me if I don't hold my breath.

Jack wondered if it would do any good to tell him that Bondy hadn't been fired— that, in a way, he was still very much with the freak show. But that would only endanger the big dumb kid.

Hank ranted on. "And if he don't come back, I'll getcha myself. And that Sharkman too!"

No you won't. Because I'm going to get it first.

4

One final trip back to the freak show.

Jack's tentative plan was to drive across the grass in the darkness and pull right up to the tent, duck under the flap, splash Scar-lip with gas, light a match, and send it back to hell.

But as he took the narrow road out to the marsh, he began to feel a crawling sensation in his gut.

Where were the tents?

Slewed his car to a halt on the muddy meadow and stared in disbelief at the empty space before his headlights. Jumped out and looked around. Gone. Hadn't passed them on the road. Where—?

Heard a sound and whirled to find a gnarled figure standing on the far side of his car. In the backwash from the headlights he could make out a grizzled and unshaven old man, but not much more.

"If you're looking for the show, you're a little late. But don't worry. They'll be back next year."

"Did you see them go?"

"Course," he said. "But not before I collected my rent."

"Do you know where—?"

"M'name's Haskins. I own this land, y'know, and you're on it."

Jack's patience was fraying. "I'll be glad to get off it, just tell me—"

"I rent it out every year to that show. They really seem to like Monroe. But I—"

"I need to know where they went."

"You're a little old to be wantin' to run off with the circus, ain't you?" he said with a wheezy laugh.

That did it. *"Where did they go?"*

"Take it easy," the old guy said. "No need for shouting. They're makin' the jump to Jersey. They open in Cape May tomorrow night."

Jack ran back to his car. South Jersey. Only a couple of possible routes for a caravan of trucks and trailers: the Cross Bronx Expressway to the George Washington Bridge would take them too far north; the Beltway to the Verrazano and across Staten Island would drop them into Central

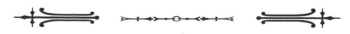

Jersey. That was the logical route. But even if he was wrong, the only way to Cape May was via the Garden State Parkway.

Jack gunned the car and headed there, figuring sooner or later he'd catch up to them.

5

Took Jack two frustrating hours just to reach Jersey. Midnight had come and gone and Cape May was still better than a hundred miles away. The limit on the Parkway along here was sixty-five. He set the cruise control on seventy and kept his foot off the gas pedal. If he had his way he'd be doing ninety, but that could put a cop on his tail and the last thing he needed was a cop.

His head ached. He'd had the radio on earlier and some station had played "You Keep Me Hanging On." Now it kept droning through his brain, Diana Ross's voice like a power saw hitting a nail.

He'd figured a train of freak show

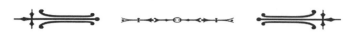

trucks and trailers would be next to impossible to miss, but he damn near did. He was a good hundred yards past the New Gretna rest stop when something familiar about the motley assortment of vehicles clustered in the southern end of the parking lot registered in his consciousness.

He slowed, found an OFFICIAL USE ONLY cut-off, and made an illegal U-turn across the median onto the northbound lanes. Half a minute later he pulled into the rest area and found a parking spot near the Burger King / Nathan's / TCBY sign where he had a good view of the freak show vehicles.

At this hour on a Wednesday morning in May, the rest area was fairly deserted. Except for a few couples straggling back from Atlantic city, Oz's folk had the lot pretty much to themselves. But why this rest area of all places? This was the only one Jack knew of that had a State Police barracks for a neighbor.

But he'd come this far…

Jack opened the trunk and stared at the gasoline can. Then he pulled a silenced

P98 .22 from where he'd hidden it beneath the spare. Teeny-tiny caliber, but at least it was quiet. He stuck it in the waistband under his warm-up and walked toward the Oddity Emporium vehicles.

Counted two eighteen-wheelers and twenty or so trailers and motor homes of various shapes and sizes and states of repair. As he neared he heard hammering sounds; seemed to come from one of the semi trailers. Two of the dog-faced roustabouts stepped from behind a motor home as Jack reached the perimeter of the cluster. They growled a warning and pointed back toward the food court.

"I want to see Oz."

More growls and more emphatic pointing.

"Look, he either gets a visit from me or I walk over to the State Police barracks there and have *them* pay him a visit."

The roustabouts didn't seem to feature that idea. Looked at each other, then one hurried away. A moment later he was back. Motioned Jack to follow. Jack lowered the zipper on his warm-up top to give him

quicker access to the P-98, then started moving.

One of the roustabouts stayed behind. As Jack followed the other on a winding course through the haphazardly parked vehicles, he saw a crew of workers trying to patch a hole in the flank of one of the semi trailers. He pulled up short when he saw the size of the hole: five or six feet high, a couple of feet wide. The edges of the metal skin were flared outward, as if a giant fist had punched through from within. And Jack was pretty sure that fist had been cobalt blue with yellow eyes.

Shit! He closed his eyes and slammed his fists against his thighs. He wanted to break something. What *else* could go wrong?

The roustabout had stopped ahead and was motioning him to hurry. Jack did just that, and soon came to the trailer he recognized as Oz's. The man himself was standing before it, watching the repair work on the truck.

"It got loose, didn't it?" Jack said as he came up beside him.

The taller man rotated the upper half of his body and looked at Jack. His expression was anything but welcoming.

"Oh, it's you. You do get around."

"Had to feed it, didn't you? Had to bring it up to full strength. Damn it, you knew the risk you were taking."

"It was caged with iron bars. I thought—"

"You thought wrong. I warned you. I've seen that thing at full strength. Iron or not, that cage wasn't going to hold it."

"I admire your talent for stating the obvious."

"Where is it?"

For the first time Jack detected a trace of fear in Oz's eyes.

"I don't know."

"Swell." He glanced around. "Where's that guy Hank?"

"Hank? What could you want with that imbecile?"

"Just wondering if he was bothering it again."

The boss slammed a bony fist into a palm. "I thought he'd learned his lesson.

Well, he'll learn it now." He turned and called into the night. "Everyone—find Hank! Find him and bring him to me at once!"

They waited but no one brought Hank. Hank was nowhere to be found.

"It appears he's run off," Prather said.

"Or got carried off."

"We found no blood near the truck, so perhaps the young idiot is still alive."

"He is alive," said a woman's voice.

Jack turned and recognized the three-eyed fortune teller from the show.

"What do you see, Carmella?" Oz said.

"He is in the woods. He stole one of the guns and he carries a spear. He is full of wine and hate. He is going to kill it."

"Oh, I doubt that," Oz said. "Going to get himself killed is more likely."

Jack understood taking a gun, but not the spear, then he remembered the pointed iron rod Hank and Bondy had used to torture it. Neither would do the job. If Hank ever caught up with the rakosh, he wouldn't last long.

He stared at the mass of trees rising on

the far side of the Parkway. "We've got to find it."

"Yes," Oz said. "Poor thing, alone out there in a strange environment, disoriented, lost, afraid."

Jack couldn't imagine Scar-lip afraid of anything, especially anything it might run across around here.

"Where'd the rakosh break out?"

"About a mile back. Right near mile marker fifty-one-point-three, to be exact. We stopped but could not stay parked on the shoulder—we'd have had the police asking what happened—so we pulled in here."

"We've got to find it."

"Nothing I'd like better, although I have a feeling you'd prefer to see it dead."

"Very perceptive."

"An interesting area here," Oz said. "Right on the edge of the Pine Barrens."

Jack cursed under his breath. The Barrens. Shit. How was he going to locate Scar-lip in there—if that was where it was? This whole area was like a time warp. Near the coast you had a nuclear power plant

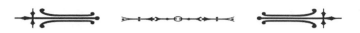

and determinedly quaint but unquestionably twentieth century towns like
Smithville and Leeds Point. West of the
Parkway was wilderness. The Barrens—a
million or so unsettled acres of pine, scrub
brush, vanished towns, hills, bogs, creeks,
all pretty much unchanged in population
and level of civilization from the time the
Indians had the Americas to themselves.
From the Revolutionary days on, it had
served as a haven for people who didn't
want to be found. Hessians, Tories, smug-
glers, Lenape Indians, heretical Amish,
escaped cons—at one time or another,
they'd all sought shelter in the Pine
Barrens.

And now add a rakosh to its long list of
fugitives.

"We're not too far from Leeds Point,
you know," Prather said, an amused
expression flitting across his sallow face.
"The birthplace of the Jersey Devil."

"Save the history lesson for later. Are
you sending out a search party?"

"No. No one wants to go, and I can't
say I blame them. But even if some were

willing, we've got to be set up in Cape May tonight for our show tomorrow."

"That leaves me."

If Scar-lip got too much of a head start, he'd never find it...which Jack could live with unless the drive to kill Vicky was still fixed in its dim brain. Seemed unlikely, but Jack couldn't take the chance.

"You're not seriously thinking of going after it."

Jack shrugged. "Know somebody who'll do it for me?"

"May I ask why?" Oz said.

"Take too long to tell. Let's just leave it that Scar-lip and I go back a ways, and we've got some unfinished business."

Oz stared at him a moment, then turned and began walking back toward his trailer.

"Come with me. Perhaps I can help."

Jack doubted that, but followed and waited outside as Oz rummaged within his trailer. Finally he emerged holding something that looked like a Gameboy. He tapped a series of buttons, eliciting a beep, then handed it to Jack.

"This will lead you to the rakosh."

Jack checked out the thing: a small screen with a blip of green light blinking slowly in one corner. He rotated his body and the blip moved.

"This is the rakosh? What'd you do—rig it with a LoJack?"

"In a way. I have electronic tell-tales on our animals. Occasionally one gets loose and I've found this to be an excellent way to track them. Most of them are irreplaceable."

"Yeah. Not too many two-headed goats wandering around."

"Correct. The range is only two miles, however. As you can see, the creature is still within range, but may not be for long. Operation is simple: Your position is center screen; if the blip is left of center, the creature is to the left of you; below center, it's behind you, and so on. You track it by proceeding in whatever direction moves the blip closer to the center of the screen. When it reaches dead center, you'll have found your rakosh. Or rather, it will have found you."

Jack swiveled back and forth until the locator blip was at the top of the faintly glowing screen. He looked up and found himself facing the shadowy mass of trees west of the Parkway. Just as he'd feared: Scar-lip was in the pines.

But this'll help me find it, he thought.

And then something occurred to him.

"You're being awfully helpful."

"Not at all. My sole concern is for the rakosh."

"But you know I'm going to kill it if I find it."

"*Try* to kill it. The pines are full of deer and other game, but the rakosh can't use them for food. As you know, it eats only one thing."

Now Jack understood. "And you think by giving me this locator, you're sending it a care package, so to speak."

Oz inclined his head. "So to speak."

"We shall see, Mr. Prather. We shall see."

"On the contrary, I doubt anyone will ever see you again."

"I'm not suicidal, trust me on that."

"But you can't believe you can take on a rakosh single-handed and survive."

"Wouldn't be the first time."

Jack headed for his car, relishing the look of concern on Oz's face before he'd turned away. Had he sounded confident enough? Good act. Because he was feeling anything but.

Jack hurried to the food area and bought half a dozen bottles of Snapple, plus an Atlantic City souvenir T-shirt, a ciggy lighter, and a newspaper. Then he moved his car to a far corner of the rest area by the RIDESHARE INFO sign and emptied the Snapple bottles onto the asphalt.

Shame to waste the stuff but it seemed Snapple was about the only thing that came in glass bottles these days.

He pulled a glasscutter from his burglary kit and began scoring the flanks of the bottles. A trick he'd learned from an old revolutionary. Upped the chances these babies would shatter on contact.

He began tearing up the shirt. Then he opened the trunk and fished out the gas can and a flashlight. He filled the bottles with gas and recapped them.

67

He gently placed the six gasoline-filled bottles into a canvas shoulder bag and worked sections of newspaper between them to keep them from clinking, then threw the pieces of T-shirt on top.

6

Jack trained his flashlight beam on the scrub at the base of the slope. He'd crossed the southbound lanes and trotted down to the 51.3 mile marker and stopped at the tree line. He was looking for broken branches and found them. Lots of them. Something big had torn through here not long ago.

He stepped through and followed the path of destruction. When he was sure he was out of sight of the highway, he stopped and pulled out the electronic locator. He was facing west and the blip was at the top edge of the screen. Had to move. Scar-lip was almost out of range.

He pressed forward until he came to a narrow path. A deer trail, most likely.

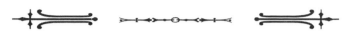

Flashed his beam down and saw what looked like deer tracks in the damp sand, but they weren't alone: deep imprints of big, alien, three-toed feet, and work-boot prints coming after. Scar-lip, with Hank following—obviously behind because the boot prints occasionally stepped on the rakosh tracks.

What's Hank thinking? Jack wondered. That he's got a gun and maybe he learned how to hunt when he was a kid, so that makes him a match for the Sharkman?

Maybe he *wasn't* thinking. Maybe a belly full of Mad Dog had convinced him he could handle the equivalent of taking on a great white with a penknife in a sea of ink.

Jack began following the deer trail, keeping one eye on the locator and turning his flashlight beam on and off every so often to check the ground. Scrub pines closed in, forming a twenty- to thirty-foot wall around him, arching their branches over the trail, allowing only an occasional glimpse of the starlit sky.

Quiet. Just the sound of insects and the branches brushing against his clothes. Jack

hated the great outdoors. Give him a city with cars and buses and honking cabs, with pavements and right angles and subways rumbling beneath his feet. And best of all—streetlights. It wasn't just dark out here, it was *dark*.

His adrenaline was up but despite the alien surroundings, he felt curiously relaxed. The locator gave him a buffer zone of safety. He knew where Scar-lip was and didn't have to worry about it jumping out of the bushes at any second and tearing into him. But he did have to worry about Hank. An armed drunk in the woods could be a danger to anything that moved. Didn't want to be mistaken for Scar-lip.

The trail wound this way and that, briefly meandering north and south, but taking him generally westward. Jack moved as fast as the circumstances allowed, making his best time along the occasional brief straightaway.

The green blip that was Scar-lip gradually moved nearer and nearer the center of the locator screen. Looked like the creature had stopped moving.

Why? Resting? Or waiting?

He guesstimated he was about a quarter mile from the rakosh when a gun report somewhere ahead brought him up short. Sounded like a shotgun. There it was again. And again.

And then a scream of fear and mortal agony echoed through the trees, rising toward a shriek that cut off sharply before it peaked.

Silence.

Jack had thought the woods quiet before, but now even the insects had shut up. He waited for other sounds. None came. And the blip on the locator showed no movement.

That pretty much told the story: Scar-lip had sensed it was being followed so it hunkered down and waited. Who comes along but one of the guys who used it as a pincushion when it was caged. Chomp-chomp, crunch-crunch, good-bye, Hank.

Jack's tongue was dry as felt. That could have—most likely would have—been him if he'd gone after Scar-lip without the locator.

But that's not the way it's going to play. I know where you are, pal, so no nasty surprises for me.

He crept ahead, and the crack and crunch of every twig and leaf he stepped on sounded amplified through a stadium PA. But Scar-lip was staying put—eating, perhaps?—so Jack kept moving.

When the blip was almost center screen, Jack stopped. He smelled something and flashed his light along the ground.

The otherwise smooth sand was kicked up ferociously for a space of about a dozen feet, ending with two large, oblong gouts of blood, drying thick and dark red, with little droplets of the same speckled all around them. A twelve-gauge Mossberg pump action lay in the brush at the edge of the trail, its wooden stock shattered.

Only one set of prints led away—the three-toed kind.

Jack crouched in the scrub grass, staring around, listening, looking for signs of movement. Nothing. But he knew from the locator that Scar-lip was dead ahead, and not too far.

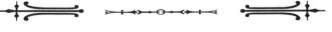

Waiting to do to me what he did to Hank, no doubt. Sorry, pal. We're gonna play it my way this time.

He removed two Snapple bottles from the shoulder bag and unscrewed their caps. Gasoline fumes rose around him as he stuffed a piece of T-shirt into the mouth of each. Lifted one, lit the rag with a little butane lighter he'd picked up along with everything else, and tossed it straight ahead along the trail.

The small flame at its mouth traced a fiery arc through the air. Before it hit the ground and *whoomph*ed into an explosion of flame, Jack had the second one in hand, ready to light.

Muscles tight, heart pounding, Jack blinked in the sudden glare as his eyes searched out the slightest sign of move-ment. Wavering shadows from the flick-ering light of the flames made *everything* look like it was moving. But nothing big and dark and solid appeared.

Something small and shiny glittered on a branch just this side of the flames. Warily Jack approached it. His foot slipped on

something along the way: The sharpened steel rod Bondy had used to torment the rakosh lay half-buried in the sand. He picked that up and carried it in his left hand like a spear. He had two weapons now. He felt like an Indian hunter, armed with an iron spear and a container of magic burning liquid.

Closer to the flames now, he stepped over a fallen log and his foot landed on something soft and yielding. Glanced down and saw a very dead Hank staring up at him through glazed eyes. He let out an involuntary yelp and jumped back.

After glancing around to make sure this wasn't a trap, he took another look at Hank. Firelight glimmered in dead blue eyes that were fixed on the stars; the pallor of Hank's bloodless face accentuated the dark rims of his shiners and blended almost perfectly with the sand under his head; his throat was a red pulpy hole and his right arm was missing at the shoulder.

Jack swallowed hard. *That could be me soon if I don't watch it.*

Stepped over him and kept moving.

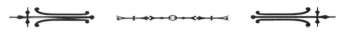

The fire from the Molotov cocktail was burning low when he reached the branch. Some of the brush had caught fire but the flames weren't spreading. Still they cast enough light to allow him to identify the shiny object.

Scar-lip's telltale collar.

Jack whirled in near panic, alarm clamoring along his adrenalized nerves as he lit the second cocktail and scanned the area for signs of the rakosh.

Nothing stirred.

This was bad, *very* bad. In the middle of nowhere and he'd given himself away with the first bomb. Now tables were reversed: Scar-lip knew exactly where Jack was, while Jack was lost in the dark with only four cocktails left.

Dark…that was the big problem. If he could find a safe place to hide for a few hours, the rising sun would level the playing field a little. But where?

Looked around and fixed on a big tree towering above the pines ahead. That might be the answer.

Jack tossed away the locator and

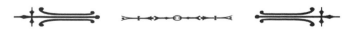

hooked the straps of the canvas bag around his shoulders, knapsack style. Spear in one hand, burning Molotov in the other, he edged ahead in a half crouch, ready to spring in any direction. Sweat trickled down his back as he swung his gaze back and forth, watching, listening, but heard nothing beyond his own harsh, ragged breaths and his racing pulse drumming in his ears.

Hopped over the dying flames of the first Molotov and saw that the trail opened onto a small clearing with the big tree at its center. Good chance Scar-lip was somewhere in or near the clearing, maybe behind the tree trunk. One good way to find out...

Tossed the second firebomb—another flaming *whoomph!* but no sign of Scar-lip—yet. Had to get to that tree. Angled around so he could see behind it—nothing. Clearing empty.

Dropped the iron spear—it would only get in his way—and hustled over to the trunk. Began to climb.

Did rakoshi climb trees? Jack couldn't

see why not. Doubted they were afraid of heights. Kept climbing, moving as fast as his battered body allowed, ascending until the branches began to crack under his weight. Satisfied that the far heavier Scar-lip could never make it this far up, he settled down to wait.

Checked the luminescent dial on his watch: just about 3:00 A.M. When was sun up? Wished he paid more attention to things like that. Didn't matter in the city, but out here in the sticks...

Tried to find a comfortable perch but that wasn't going to happen, and a nap was out of the question. He found some solace in the realization that no way was Scar-lip going to catch him by surprise up here.

Through the leaves of the big oak he could see patches of the sandy clearing below, gray against the surrounding blackness. On the eastern horizon, a dim glow from the Parkway and the rest area; but to the west, nothing but the featureless black forever of the Pine Barrens—

Jack stiffened as he saw a light—make that two lights—moving along the treetops to the west…heading his way. At first he thought it might be a plane or helicopter, but the lights were mismatched in size and maintained no fixed relationship to each other. His second thought was UFOs, but these didn't appear to be objects at all. They looked like globules of light…light and nothing more.

He'd heard of these things but had never seen one…the Pineys called them pine lights but no one knew what they were. Jack didn't want to find out and would have preferred to see them heading elsewhere. They weren't traveling a straight line—the smaller one would dart left and right, and even the larger one meandered a little. But no question about it: those two glowing blobs were heading his way.

They slowed as they reached the clearing and Jack got a closer look at them. He didn't like what he saw. One was basketball size, the other maybe a bit larger than a softball. Light shouldn't form into a ball; it wasn't right. Something unhealthy about the pale green color too.

Jack cringed as they came straight for

the tree, fearing they were going to touch him—something about them made his skin crawl—but they split within half a dozen feet of the branches. He heard a high-pitched hum and felt his skin tingle as they skirted his perch to the north and south. They paired up again on the far side but instead of moving on, spiraled down toward the clearing.

Jack craned his neck to see where they were going. Toward Hank's body? No, that was on the north side of the tree. They were moving the other way.

He watched them hover over an empty patch of sand, then begin to chase each other in a tight circle—slowly at first, then with increasing speed until they blurred into a glowing ring, an unholy halo of wan green light, moving faster and faster, the centrifugal force of their rising speed widening the ring until they shot off into the night, racing back toward the west where they'd come from.

Good riddance. The whole episode had lasted perhaps a minute, but left him unsettled. Wondered if this happened every

night, or if Scar-lip's presence had anything to do with it.

And speaking of Scar-lip…

Checked the clearing as best he could
through the intervening foliage, but still
nothing stirred.

Tried to settle down again and make
plans for sunrise….

7

Jack didn't wait for full light. The stars
had begun to fade around four-thirty. By
five, although still probably half an hour
before the sun officially rose, the pewter
sky was bright enough for him to feel comfortable quitting the Tarzan scene and
heading back to earth.

Stiff and sore, he eased himself toward
the ground, continually checking the
clearing—still empty except for Hank.
Soon as he hit the sand he opened the
Snapple bottles and stuffed their mouths
with rag. He kept one in hand and held the
lighter ready.

The plan was simple: Start at Hank's corpse and follow Scar-lip's footprints from there. He'd keep it up as long as he could. Didn't know how long he could go without food and water, but he'd give it his best shot. Right now what he wanted most was a cup of coffee.

As he approached the corpse, he noticed that the pinelands insects hadn't been idle: flies taxied around Hank's head while ants partied in the throat wound and shoulder stump. The thought of burying him crossed Jack's mind, but he had neither the time nor the tools.

A noise behind him. Jack whirled. Put down the bag and thumbed the flint wheel on the butane lighter as he scanned the clearing in the pallid predawn light.

There…on the far side, the spot where the pine lights had done their little dervish a couple of hours ago, a patch of sand, moving, shifting, rising. No, not sand. This was very big and very dark.

Scar-lip.

Jack took an involuntary step back, then held his ground. The rakosh wasn't moving; it simply stood there, maybe thirty feet away, where it had buried itself for the night. Hank's arm dangled from its three-fingered right hand; Scar-lip held it casually, like a lollipop. The upper half of the arm had been stripped of its flesh; sand coated the pink bone.

Jack felt his gut tighten, his heart turning in overdrive. Here was his chance. He lit the tail on the cocktail and stepped over the shoulder bag, straddling it. Slowly he bent, pulled out a second bomb, and lit it from the first.

Had to get this right the first time. He knew from past encounters how quick and agile these creatures were in spite of their mass. But he also knew that all he had to do was hit it with one of these flaming babies and it would all be over.

With no warning and as little wind-up as he dared, he tossed the Molotov in his right hand. The rakosh ducked away, as expected, but Jack was ready with the other…gave it a left-handed heave, leading the rakosh, trying to catch it on the run. Both missed. The first landed in an explo-

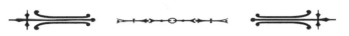

sion of flame, but the second skidded on the sand and lay there intact, its fuse dead, smothered.

As the rakosh shied away from the flames, Jack pulled out a third cocktail. His heart stuttered, his hand shook, and he'd just lit the fuse when he sensed something hurtling toward him through dimness, close, too close. Ducked but not soon enough. The twirling remnant of Hank's arm hit him square in the face.

Coughing in revulsion as he sprawled back, Jack felt the third cocktail slip from his fingers. He turned and dived and rolled. He was clear when it exploded, but he kept rolling because it had landed on the shoulder bag. He felt a blast of heat as his last Molotov went up.

As soon as the initial explosion of flame subsided, Scar-lip charged across the clearing. Jack was still on his back in the sand. Instinct prompted his hand toward the P-98 but he knew bullets were useless. Spotted the iron spear beside him, grabbed it, swung it around so the butt was in the dirt and the point toward the onrushing rakosh. His mind flashed back to his apartment rooftop last summer when Scar-lip's mother was trying to kill him, when he had run her through. That had only slowed her then, but this was iron. Maybe this time....

He steadied the point and braced for the impact.

The impact came, but not the one he'd expected. In one fluid motion, Scar-lip swerved and batted the spear aside, sending it sailing away through the air toward the oak. Jack was left flat on his back with a slavering, three-hundred-pound inhuman killing machine towering over him. Tried to roll to his feet but the rakosh caught him with its foot and pinned him to the sand. As Jack struggled to slip free, Scar-lip increased the pressure, eliciting live wires of agony from his cracking ribs. Stretched to reach the P-98. Spitballs would probably damage a rakosh as much as .22s, but that was all he had left. And no way was he going out with a fully loaded pistol. Maybe if he went for the eyes...

But before he could pull the pistol free of his warm-up pocket, he saw Scar-lip

raise its right hand, spread the three talons wide, then drive them toward his throat.

No time to prepare, no room to dodge, he simply cried out in terror in what he was sure would be the last second of his life.

But the impact was not the sharp tearing pain of a spike ramming through his flesh. Instead he choked as the talons speared the sand to either side and the web between them closed off his wind. The pressure eased from his chest but the talons tightened, encircling his throat as he struggled for air. And then Jack felt himself yanked from the sand and held aloft, kicking and twisting in the silent air, flailing ineffectually at the flint-muscled arm that gripped him like a vise. The popping of the vertebral joints in his neck sounded like explosions, the cartilage in his larynx whined under the unremitting pressure as the rakosh shook him like an abusive parent with a baby who had cried once too often, and all the while his lungs pleaded, *screamed* for air.

His limbs quickly grew heavy, the oxygen-starved muscles weakening until

he could no longer lift his arms. Black spots flashed and floated in the space between him and Scar-lip as his panicked brain's clawhold on consciousness began to falter. Life…he could feel his life slipping away, the universe fading to gray…and he was floating…gliding aloft toward—

—a jarring impact, sand in his face, in his mouth, but air too, good Christ, *air!*

He lay gasping, gulping, coughing, retching, but breathing, and slowly light seeped back to his brain, life to his limbs.

Jack lifted his head, looked around. Scar-lip not in sight. Rolled over, looked up. Scar-lip nowhere.

Slowly, hesitantly, he raised himself on his elbows, amazed to be alive. But how long would that last? So weak. And God, he hurt.

Looked around again. Blinked. Alone in the clearing.

What was going on here? Was the rakosh hiding, waiting to pop out again and start playing with him like a cat with a captured mouse?

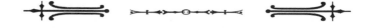

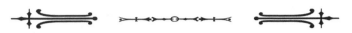

He struggled to his knees but stopped there until the pounding in his head eased. Looked around once more, baffled. Still no sign of Scar-lip.

What the hell?

Cautiously Jack rose to his feet and braced for a dark shape to hurtle from the brush and finish him off.

Nothing moved. The rakosh was gone.

Why? Nothing here to frighten it off, and it sure as hell wasn't turning vegetarian, because Hank's arm, the one Scar-lip had thrown at Jack, was missing.

Jack turned in a slow circle. Why didn't it kill me?

Because he'd stopped Bondy and Hank from torturing it? Not possible. A rakosh was a killing machine. What would it know about fair play, about debts or gratitude? Those were human emotions and—

Then Jack remembered that Scar-lip was part human. Kusum Bahkti had been its father. It carried some of Kusum in it and, despite some major leaks in his skylights, Kusum had been a stand-up guy.

Was that it? If so, the Otherness prob-

ably wanted to disown Scar-lip. But its daddy might be proud.

Jack's instincts were howling for him to go—*now*. But he held back. He'd come here to finish this, and he'd failed. Utterly. The rakosh was back to full strength and roaming free in the trackless barrens.

But maybe it *was* finished—at least between Scar-lip and him. Maybe the last rakosh was somebody else's problem now. Not that he could do anything about Scar-lip anyway. As much as he hated to leave a rakosh alive and free here in the wild, he didn't see that he had much choice. He'd been beaten. Worse than beaten: he'd been hammered flat and kicked aside like an old tin can. He had no useful weapons left, and Scar-lip had made it clear that Jack was no match one on one.

Time to call it quits. At least for today. But he couldn't let it go, not without one last shot.

"Listen," he shouted, wondering if the creature could hear him, and how much it would understand. "I guess we're even. We'll leave it this way. For now. But if you

ever threaten me or mine again, I'll be back. And I won't be carrying Snapple bottles."

Jack began to edge toward the trail, but kept his face to the clearing, still unable to quite believe this, afraid if he turned his back the creature would rise out of the sand and strike.

As soon as Jack reached the trail, he turned and started moving as fast as his hip allowed. A last look over his shoulder before the pines and brush obscured the clearing showed what looked like a dark, massive figure standing alone on the sand, surveying its new domain. But when Jack stopped for a better look, it was gone.

8

He got himself lost on the way out. His defeat and release had left him bewildered and a little dazed, neither of which had helped his concentration. A low lid of overcast added to the problem. The trail forked here and there and he knew he wanted to keep heading east, but he couldn't be sure where that was without the sun to fix on.

Even so, he didn't want to be caught carrying when he reached the road. He pulled the P-98 from his pocket and opened the breech. He ejected the clip and, using his thumbnail, flicked the .22 long rifles free one by one, sending them flying in all directions. He tossed the empty clip into the brush. Then he kicked a hole in the sand, dropped the pistol into the depression, and smoothed sand back over it with his foot.

The gun was lousy with his fingerprints, but after a couple of rainstorms in this acid soil, that wouldn't be a problem. No one was going to find it out here anyway.

He walked on, and the extra traveling time gave him room to think.

I blew it.

Defeat weighed on him, and he knew that wasn't right. The notion of Scar-lip roaming free was a bone in his throat that he could neither cough up nor swallow. He felt some sort of obligation to let it be known that something big and dangerous

was prowling the Pine Barrens. But how? He couldn't personally go public with the story, and who'd believe him anyway?

He was still trying to come up with a solution when he heard faint voices off to his right. He angled toward them.

The brush opened up and he found himself facing a worn two-lane blacktop. A couple of SUVs were parked on the sandy shoulder where four men, thirty to forty in age, were busily loading shotguns and slipping into day-glo orange vests. Their gear was expensive, top of the line, their weapons Remingtons and Berettas. Gentlemen sportsmen, out for the kill.

Jack asked which way to the Parkway and they pointed off to the left.

A guy with a dainty goatee gave him a disdainful up-and-down.

"What'd you run into? A bear?"

"Worse."

"You could get killed walking through the woods like that, you know," another said, a skinny guy with glasses. "Someone might pop you if you aren't wearing colors."

"I'll be sticking to the road from here on." Curiosity got the better of Jack. "What're you hunting with all that firepower?"

"Deer," the goatee replied. "The State Wildlife Department's ordered a special off-season harvest."

"Harvest, ay? Sounds like you're talking wheat instead of deer."

"Might as well be, considering the way the herd's been growing. There's just too damn many deer out there for their own good."

A balding guy grinned. "And we're doing our civic and ecological duty by thinning the herd."

Jack hesitated, then figured he ought to give these guys a heads-up. "Maybe you want to think twice about going in there today."

"Shit," said the balding one, his grin vanishing. "You're not one of those animal rights creeps are you?"

The air suddenly bristled with hostility.

"I'm not *any* kind of creep, pal," Jack said through his teeth. Barely into the

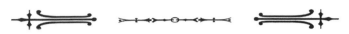

morning and already his fuse was down to a nubbin; he took faint satisfaction in seeing the jerk step back up and tighten his grip on his shotgun. "I'm just telling you there's something real mean wandering around in there."

"Like what?" said the goatee, smirking. "The Jersey Devil?"

"No. But it's not some defenseless herbivore that's going to lay down and die when you empty a couple of shells at it. As of today, guys, you're no longer at the top of the food chain in the pines."

"We can handle it," said the skinny one.

"Really?" Jack said. "When did you ever hunt something that posed the slightest threat to you? I'm just warning you, there's something in there that fights back and I doubt any of your type can handle that."

Skinny looked uneasy now. He glanced at the others. "What if he's right?"

"Oh, shit!" said baldy. "You going pussy on us, Charlie? Gonna let some tree-hugger chase you off with spook stories?"

"Well, no, but—"

The fourth hunter hefted a shiny new Remington over-under.

"The Jersey Devil! I want it! Wouldn't that be some kind of head to hang over the fireplace?"

They all laughed, and Charlie joined in, back in the fold again as they slapped each other high fives.

Jack shrugged and walked away. He'd tried.

Hunting season. Had to smile. Scar-lip's presence in the Pine Barrens gave the term a whole new twist. He wondered how these mighty hunters would react when they learned that the season was open on *them.*

And he wondered if there'd been any truth to those old tales of the Jersey Devil. Most likely hadn't been a real Jersey Devil before, but there sure as hell was now.